W9-CCE-526

Noah's Noisy Night

by Maria Correa

Illustrated by Sebastien Braun

It had been a VERY busy day on Noah's ark.
At last, all the animals lay snug in their beds
as the rain fell pitter-patter.

"Sweet dreams, everyone," yawned Mrs. Noah,
climbing into bed.

Noah had just started to snore when a loud

BOO-HOO

woke him up with a jump.

"What a racket!" he cried.
It was the bears.
"We can't sleep!" they sniffed. "It's too dark!"

So Noah gave each of them a big bear hug,
and a night-light to glow softly in the dark.

He tiptoed back to his room, but then he heard a
CREAK and a CRASH.

"Crinkly whiskers! What a ruckus," he said.
It was the crocodiles arguing.
"I want the top bunk!" one shouted.
"It's mine!" yelled the other.

TROPICAL
ECOLOGY

Noah stacked some boxes—1, 2, 3—until
there were TWO top bunks. Hooray!

With the
crocodiles sleeping
side by side, he started
back to his room when he heard a

FLAP and a HONK.

"Oh, dear," he sighed.
"We can't sleep!" squeaked the penguins. "It's too hot!"
So Noah gave them a nice ice bath.
Splish, splash, splosh!

Soon they were cool and ready for bed.
"Now, sleep ti–," Noah started to say when he heard a big

THUMP!

"Oh, goodness!" cried Noah. "What now?"
The giraffes were galloping back and forth.
"Woo-hoo!" they laughed,
much too excited to sleep.

Then **clatter**! fell a mop and **whoosh**! flew a book, **SMASH!**

CLATTER! BANG!

"Oh, no!" Noah gasped.
At first, it was quiet. Then there was a honk,
and then a roar, a stomp, and a thunder of feet . . .
and ALL of the animals rushed through the door.

Plan a ↓

"Now I'll NEVER get any sleep!" wailed Noah.

Just then, Mrs. Noah appeared.
"Oh, my! You're all wide awake," she said.
"I know what you need."

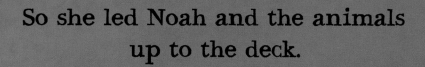

So she led Noah and the animals
up to the deck.

The rain had stopped, and the stars twinkled.
The animals cuddled close as Mrs. Noah
read them a bedtime story.

Noah was the first one to start snoring.
And the animals followed, dozing off two by two.
"Sweet dreams, everyone," smiled Mrs. Noah.
And with a yawn, she fell fast asleep, too.

For my wee pals Noah, Ellis, and Joshua. — M.C.

For Ben, Joey, Elijah, Naomi. — S.B.

tiger tales

5 River Road, Suite 128, Wilton, CT 06897
Published in the United States 2019
Originally published in Great Britain 2019
by Little Tiger Press Ltd.
Text by Maria Correa
Text copyright © 2019 Little Tiger Press Ltd.
Illustrations copyright © 2019 Sebastien Braun
ISBN-13: 978-1-68010-132-4
ISBN-10: 1-68010-132-3
Printed in China
LTP/1800/2396/0918
10 9 8 7 6 5 4 3 2 1

For more insight and activities, visit us at www.tigertalesbooks.com